BEYBLADE

OFFICIAL HANDBOOK

METAL FUSION AND METAL MASTERS

BY TRACEY WEST

ISBN 978-0-545-43386-0

©Takafumi Adachi, MFBBProject, TV Tokyo

Licensed by/Licencié par d-rights Inc.

Representative/Représentant – Nelvana International Limited

Published by Scholastic Inc. All rights reserved.

SCHOLASTIC and associated logos are trademarks and/or registered trademarks of Scholastic Inc.

12 11 10 9 8 7 6 5 4 3 2   13 14 15 16 17/0

Printed in the U.S.A.   40

First printing, January 2012

Special thanks to
Alexander, Dylan, and Ryan R.

SCHOLASTIC INC.
New York • Toronto • London • Auckland
Sydney • Mexico City • New Delhi • Hong Kong

LET IT RIP! ™

Does the sound of a spinning top make you cheer? Do you dream of Beyblade battles in your sleep? Is your Beyblade collection the most organized thing in your bedroom?

If you answered "yes" to any of these questions, then you've got the heart of a true Beyblade Blader. This is the book for you.

In these pages, you'll meet the heroes and rivals of Beyblade. You'll get info on your favorite Beys — and maybe even meet some you didn't know existed. You'll also get advice on how to become a master competitor, just like the world's number one Blader: Gingka Hagane.

By the time you finish this book, you'll be ready to battle with the best of them. So what are you waiting for? レット イット リップ

LET IT RIP! ™

THE LEGEND OF

Long ago, a shining meteor streaked through the sky. It struck the sleepy village of Koma, Japan, leaving a huge, hollowed-out crater in the earth. People were awed by the pure, positive light shining from the meteorite.

At the same time, in a far-off land, another meteor fell. But this one contained a power that was evil. Bewitched by that power, the people in that far-off village used a piece of the meteorite to create an evil spinning top — the very first Bey.

The first Bey absorbed the negative feelings of the villagers and turned it into a dark power. As time passed, the Bey stored up dark power and changed shape to become the Bey known as Lightning L-Drago.

When the people of Koma Village heard about L-Drago, they used a piece of their meteorite to create a Bey that carried the light of the people's hope. This Bey, Pegasus, fought a fierce battle with L-Drago. Pegasus prevailed, and L-Drago was sealed away in Koma Village. It became known as "The Forbidden Bey."

BEYBLADE

From that moment on, Beyblade spread throughout the world. The crater in Koma Village became the first stadium. More Beys were made using the same positive energy that filled Pegasus. Bladers challenged one another in tournaments to test their skills — and have fun.

It was believed that L-Drago would remain hidden in Koma Village forever. **But then a dark force arrived in Koma . . . and threatened to change the world of Beyblade forever.**

GET A GRIP!

BEYBLADE METAL FUSION

"**Three . . . two . . . one . . . LET IT RIP!**™"

The sound of Beyblade battles beginning could be heard all over the world. Bladers faced one another to practice, challenged one another in informal battles, or competed in official tournaments organized by the WBBA: the World Beyblade Association.

Then the ultimate tournament was announced: Battle Bladers. Bladers all over the country competed in qualifying rounds, and those who made it entered Battle Bladers. The winner would be crowned number one Blader, a title no one had ever held before.

Gingka Hagane and his friends were eager to enter the tournament, compete in exciting battles with new opponents, and prove they had what it takes to be the best. But there was something else at stake: a shadowy force called the Dark Nebula was behind the tournament. Led by Doji, the Dark Nebula's goal was to strengthen the Forbidden Bey, Lightning L-Drago, by draining the power from Bladers and their Beys in battle.

A Blader named Ryuga controlled L-Drago. Together, it seemed like they couldn't be beat. But Gingka and his friends wouldn't give up. It was up to them to defeat Ryuga and L-Drago, or the world of Beyblade would be destroyed forever.

METAL FUSION HEROES

"A Bey battle isn't about destroying your opponent. It's about creating friendships and battling together." — Gingka

Gingka Hagane is a Blader who's hard to beat. Determined to become a better Blader, he's traveled far and wide, facing any opponents willing to battle him. From the beginning, he's been intent on defeating Doji and getting L-Drago back from Ryuga.

During his journey, Gingka made new friends. Some, like Kenta, were young Bladers who looked up to Gingka. Then there's Madoka, who lent her skills to help Gingka improve his game. Others were rivals who realized that Gingka was on the right path. Gingka even had a few mysterious friends waiting in the wings for the right time to come to the rescue.

Each of these Bladers has a strong spirit. When those spirits combined, they proved to be unstoppable!

BLADER QUOTE

"A Beyblade's true strength has nothing to do with attack power or stamina. It attacks using the feelings of the Blader who's connected with it, as if all the power in the cosmos was being poured into it. You must put your heart that is as big as the starry sky into it."

GINGKA
BEYBLADE: STORM PEGASUS

In battle, Gingka is a fearless and determined Blader. His strength comes from the fact that he has a powerful connection with his Bey, Pegasus, and he believes that a Blader must have a strong spirit to win. He learned this while growing up in Koma, known as "The Beyblade Village."

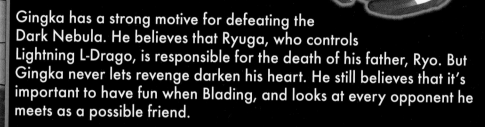

Gingka has a strong motive for defeating the Dark Nebula. He believes that Ryuga, who controls Lightning L-Drago, is responsible for the death of his father, Ryo. But Gingka never lets revenge darken his heart. He still believes that it's important to have fun when Blading, and looks at every opponent he meets as a possible friend.

DID YOU KNOW?
Gingka loves hamburgers almost as much as he loves Beyblading. When he entered the Survival Battle, he planned on asking for a twenty-layer beef burger if he won.

KYOYA
BEYBLADE: ROCK LEONE

With his sharp teeth and wild hair, Kyoya resembles the fierce lion spirit of his Bey, Rock Leone. Kyoya is the former leader of the Face Hunters, a gang of Bladers who challenged weaker opponents in order to steal points from their Beys.

Doji of the Dark Nebula forced Kyoya to go through harsh training. He had to climb a treacherous mountain and defeat a pack of wolves. The training transformed Kyoya into a dark warrior who disbanded the Face Hunters; turned his back on his best friend, Benkei; and challenged Gingka to a battle.

During the battle, Gingka helped Kyoya find his true spirit. Kyoya became one of Gingka's closest allies and joined his quest to destroy the Dark Nebula. But Kyoya still wants to face Gingka once again — and defeat him in competition.

DID YOU KNOW?
Kyoya was the first Blader to earn more than 50,000 battle points in the Battle Bladers qualifying rounds, gaining him the first slot in the tournament.

BLADER QUOTE
"Who do you think you are, buddy? I don't take orders."

KENTA
BEYBLADE: FLAME SAGITTARIO

If Gingka had a fan club, Kenta would be its president. Kenta looks up to Gingka and wants to be just like him someday. He's off to a good start. Kenta might be small and cute, but he has a brave heart.

Kenta isn't fearless, but he is courageous. He overcomes his fear to stand up to bullies and help those who need it. When creepy, crab-obsessed Tetsuya battled Kenta's friends, purposely scratching their Beys, Kenta stepped up and offered to battle Tetsuya instead. Later on, he even stood up to Doji.

Kenta can be very strong when he needs to be. When his friend Benkei was hurt during a battle with Kyoya, Kenta carried the big Blader on his back all the way across town!

DID YOU KNOW?
When Gingka was sick, Kenta pretended to be Gingka and accepted a battle challenge from Hikaru. He lost, and felt so terrible about it that he trained harder than ever. He faced Hikaru again and won.

BLADER QUOTE
"Beyblading is the best!"

BENKEI
BEYBLADE: DARK BULL

Benkei was so impressed by Kyoya's Blading abilities that he joined the Face Hunters, vowing to follow Kyoya anywhere. In battle, this big Blader charges his opponents and never backs down — just like his Bey, Dark Bull. Whenever Benkei is frustrated, angry, excited, or even happy, he yells the same thing: "Ba-ba-bull!"

He might look like a bully you don't want to mess with, but Benkei is more like a big, stuffed teddy bear. His friendship with Gingka began when they first battled, and Benkei rescued Gingka from falling debris. He saved Madoka when she was kidnapped by Tetsuya and trapped in a sandpit surrounded by crabs. And he admired Kenta's fighting spirit so much that he helped the young Blader train so he could defeat Hikaru.

Benkei's big heart helps him when he's Blading. The deep connection he has with Dark Bull makes them a pair that's tough to beat.

DID YOU KNOW?
Benkei also helped train Kenta's friends Osamu, Takashi, and Akira.

BLADER QUOTE
"I can't control this odd feeling. I'm actually being . . . nice!"

MADOKA

Madoka loves Beyblade, but she rarely battles. Instead, she prefers fixing Beys and running battle simulations on her laptop. Madoka works out of a workshop in the basement of the B-Pit, a Beyblade store owned by her father.

Madoka first met Gingka when she saw him battling and noticed that his Pegasus was damaged. She stayed up all night fixing it for him. It was clear that Madoka loves Beys and hates to see them injured.

Madoka also has a great eye in battle. She watches Beys in action and figures out what's making them perform the way they do. If you're in a battle, it's good to have Madoka by your side — once she figures out what your opponent is up to, she'll share strategies to help you win.

DID YOU KNOW?

Madoka was one of the final four contenders in the Survival Battle, a competition that was held before Battle Bladers. She only battled once during the whole event — when she threw a Bey into Kyoya's battle with Yu to prevent Rock Leone from becoming damaged.

BLADER QUOTE

"Remember to be good to your Beys and they'll be good to you."

HIKARU
BEYBLADE: STORM AQUARIO

Tough and determined, Hikaru learned her battle strategy from her mother, who told her to challenge only the best Bladers and never back down. Hikaru's excellent skills earned her a spot in the first round of Battle Bladers.
She was the first one to face Ryuga, of the Dark Nebula. When the two faced each other across the stadium, dark energy began to pour from Ryuga, terrifying Hikaru. In that moment, she was defeated.

DID YOU KNOW?

When Hikaru first came to town, Benkei and some Face Hunters told her she had to defeat them in order to enter. Hikaru easily beat them all with her Storm Aquario.

BLADER QUOTE

"To win against strong opponents — that is the destiny. I have been given the path I must follow."

HYOMA
BEYBLADE: ROCK ARIES

Hyoma is a childhood friend of Gingka's. The two future Bladers grew up together in Koma Village. But when Kenta, Benkei, Kyoya, and Madoka first met Hyoma, he didn't seem too friendly. He insisted that they each battle him before he'd lead them to Koma Village to find Gingka. After defeating Benkei and Kenta, Hyoma finally agreed to help them.

Despite this rocky beginning, Hyoma proved to be a good ally during Battle Bladers. He even took on Tsubasa in order to buy Gingka enough time to reach a tournament. But when Hyoma faced Reiji at Battle Bladers, he was among the first to suffer at the hands of the merciless Blader and his Poison Serpent.

BLADER QUOTE
"Don't worry, I'm not an oddball or anything."

PHOENIX
BEYBLADE: BURN FIREBLAZE

Phoenix first appeared during the Battle Bladers challenge matches, watching from the shadows. Gingka later learned that Phoenix was actually his father, Ryo. Gingka thought his father was lost after he tried to stop Ryuga from stealing L-Drago, the Forbidden Bey, from Koma village. To keep his existence a secret from the Dark Nebula, Ryo became Phoenix.

At first, Gingka didn't understand why his father kept the fact that he was alive a secret even from his own son. But once Gingka saw the horrifying dark power of L-Drago in action, he forgave Ryo. When Gingka faced Ryuga in Battle Bladers, Ryo was there to cheer him on.

DID YOU KNOW?

In mythology, the phoenix is a bird that lives for hundreds of years. Then it builds a nest of fire, burns, and comes to life once more. It's a fitting name for this mysterious masked Blader.

BLADER QUOTE

"The flame of Fireblaze melts away everything!"

TSUBASA
BEYBLADE: EARTH EAGLE

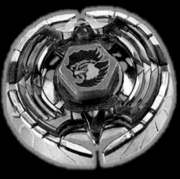

First you hear the cry of an eagle. Then you look up, and see an eagle soaring in the sky. That's when Tsubasa appears. This Blader is calm and controlled, and he appears to hold valuable Beyblade wisdom deep within him.

When Gingka was approached by Bladers who wanted to steal his battle points, Tsubasa came to his aid. He said he knew Gingka's true goal — but how?

When Tsubasa joined the Dark Nebula, it looked like he might be one of the bad guys. He was actually infiltrating the organization so he could download information on L-Drago and Ryuga, in hopes of defeating them. But even that knowledge couldn't save Tsubasa from L-Drago's unstoppable dark powers.

DID YOU KNOW?

To get the Dark Nebula to hire him, Tsubasa had to defeat three Bladers at once — the Kumade Brothers — and then go one-on-one against Yu and his powerful Flame Libra.

BLADER QUOTE

"You have to be very observant. If you are, things will become clearer."

METAL FUSION RIVALS

Each Beyblade holds a hidden power that should only be used in Bey battles. The members of the Dark Nebula are obsessed with this power, and they want to use it to control the world. That's why they stole Lightning L-Drago and broke its seal, unleashing its dark energy.

The Dark Nebula held the Battle Bladers tournament for one reason: so L-Drago could drain powerful Beys and Bladers and absorb their energy. To do that, Doji, the chief executive of the Dark Nebula, recruited a team of Bladers strong enough to take on Gingka and his friends.

The Bladers were drawn to the Dark Nebula with promises of fame or power or wealth. Many of them didn't know about Doji's evil plans. But when they found out, it was too late for some of them to save themselves . . . and the game they love.

RYUGA
BEYBLADE:
LIGHTNING L-DRAGO

Ryuga is the Blader who stole L-Drago, the Forbidden Bey, from Koma Village. When Gingka's father, Ryo, tried to stop him, Ryuga poured all his power into L-Drago to fight Ryo off. Ryuga escaped with L-Drago, but it took him a long time to recover from that battle.

Ryuga slowly gained back his power in a pod in the Dark Nebula labs. He awakened when Gingka infiltrated the Dark Nebula castle, hoping to find L-Drago and destroy it. Ryuga and Gingka battled, and Ryuga taunted Gingka about his lost father. Gingka grew angry, and that anger only made L-Drago more powerful. Gingka lost that night.

When Ryuga battles with L-Drago, he glows with evil purple energy and sometimes takes on the appearance of a dragon. In his final battle with Gingka, Ryuga actually transformed into a monster. Ryuga believed that he could control L-Drago . . . but the evil Bey was controlling him all along.

DID YOU KNOW?
Doji may have recruited Ryuga, but near the end of the Battle Bladers tournament, Ryuga decided that he didn't need Doji anymore. He drained Doji and his Dark Wolf of their power and fed it to L-Drago.

BLADER QUOTE
"As the Blader chosen by L-Drago, I am the strongest Blader in the world!"

DOJI
BEYBLADE: DARK WOLF

Doji is a powerful, wealthy man who formed the Dark Nebula so he could use the power of L-Drago to rule the world one day. Doji is cold and cruel, and he delivers harsh punishment to Bladers who work for him if they fail at the task they're given.

Doji's certain that Gingka represented the biggest threat to the Dark Nebula — and he's right. But no matter how many Bladers he sent after Gingka, he couldn't make Gingka give up.

Doji's French-speaking computer is an advanced form of artificial intelligence. Merci tricked Gingka into thinking he's on a Beyblade game show so he could test and record Gingka's abilities.

DID YOU KNOW?
Doji usually walks around drinking orange juice from a champagne glass. He enjoys eating pepperoni pizza with a knife and fork because he believes it's "more civilized."

BLADER QUOTE
"The power of Beyblades has been used to change the course of rivers and oceans. They have been used to defeat many armies and create huge empires."

YU
BEYBLADE: FLAME LIBRA

He may look and act like an adorable (and annoying) little kid, but Yu is the Dark Nebula's top Blader after Ryuga. Yu has created some amazing special moves for his Flame Libra, and he's a brilliant strategist as well.

At the Survival Battle, Yu and Gingka were the final two Bladers. Yu shocked everyone when he and his Flame Libra defeated Gingka and Pegasus with some powerful shock wave moves. But the biggest surprise came when Yu claimed his prize and wished for the Battle Bladers tournament — and everyone learned he was working for Doji.

But Yu came to respect Gingka, and he decided to leave the Dark Nebula. Doji promised him his freedom if he could defeat Reiji and his Poison Serpent. The battle ended in a huge explosion of power, and Yu ran away to seek safety with Gingka and his friends.

DID YOU KNOW?
Yu has a nickname for most of his friends. Gingka is "Gingky," Kenta is "Kenchi," Benkei is "Ben-Ben," and Kyoya is "Yo-Yo."

BLADER QUOTE
"This is gonna be fun, fun, fun. Yeah!"

TETSUYA
BEYBLADE: MAD GASHER/ DARK GASHER

Tetsuya is a creepy, wandering Blader who absolutely loves crabs. He uses the word crab in every sentence — "That's crabulous!"— and even seems to be able to control the crustaceans. So it's no surprise that his Bey, Mad Gasher, takes the form of a crab in battle.

When he was very young, Tetsuya was betrayed by a friend. Now he hates friendship and delights in making happy Bladers sad. When he's finished with a battle, he will order Mad Gasher to scratch up the defeated Beys.

Before Tetsuya joined the Dark Nebula, he showed up and started scratching up the Beys of young Bladers. When Gingka refused to battle him, he kidnapped Madoka, leaving Gingka no choice. Gingka and his Pegasus defeated Mad Gasher, leaving Tetsuya feeling very . . . crabby!

DID YOU KNOW?
Tetsuya is often called by his last name, Watarigani, which is the Japanese name for a crab.

BLADER QUOTE
"Now for a crabtastic finish!"

REIJI
BEYBLADE:
POISON SERPENT

Reiji is as cold and dangerous as the snake spirit that lives inside his Bey. His yellow eyes are strangely reptilian. He gets pleasure out of destroying his opponents and their Beys.

When he faced Hyoma, Gingka's childhood friend begged Reiji to spare his Beyblade. Reiji just smirked and refused, showing no mercy.

When Reiji first appeared at Battle Bladers, nobody could find a record of him in any database. But he ended up being one of the most dangerous opponents Gingka and his friends would face.

BLADER QUOTE
"I'll defeat you so completely that you'll never be able to pick up a Bey again."

RYUTARO

BEYBLADE: THERMAL PISCES

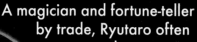

A magician and fortune-teller by trade, Ryutaro often psychs out opponents who are afraid of his unusual abilities. But there's nothing magical about his Blading skills: in a match, he has the true talent of an expert Blader. With his Thermal Pisces, he is able to create illusions that confuse his opponents.

When Ryutaro and Tobio lost a Battle Bladers challenge match to Ryuga, Ryuga invited them to join the Dark Nebula. Ryutaro believed it was his fate to join them, and he went on to face Gingka in the first round of the tournament. Gingka's fighting spirit defeated Ryutaro's illusions and, in the end, the battling magician realized that Gingka and his pure energy was the true future of Beyblade.

DID YOU KNOW?

Before Ryutaro commands Thermal Pisces to perform a special move, he says "Good luck, come my way!" three times.

BLADER QUOTE

"No matter how hard you try, the future cannot be changed."

TOBIO
BEYBLADE: STORM CAPRICORN

Tobio is a tough Blader who thinks of himself as a soldier. He is known as "Captain Capri," and he uses a lot of military jargon in battle. He likes to calculate each attack angle precisely and strategize very carefully when he's battling.

When Tobio challenged Kyoya, he was sure he'd win. But Kyoya had observed Tobio's battle strategies and was able to surprise him. After Kyoya defeated him, Tobio was determined to get stronger, so he joined the Dark Nebula.

BLADER QUOTE
"Once I have a target, I don't let it get away."

DAN AND REIKI
BEYBLADE: EVIL GEMIOS

These twins work for the Dark Nebula. When Gingka first met them, they used their Beys in combination attacks. Then Doji gave them a dark Bey, Evil Gemios, and the two Bladers controlled the single Bey in battle.

The only problem with that strategy was that the brothers couldn't agree on what to do. They were opposites, just like the Fire and Ice attacks of Evil Gemios. Reiki always wanted to attack, while Dan was more patient.

This sibling squabbling led to a crushing defeat in a Battle Bladers challenge match against Kenta. Kenta used Sagittario's Flame Claw attack to slam Evil Gemios for the win.

DID YOU KNOW?

Reiki wears a blue vest and controls the Ice moves of Evil Gemios. Dan wears a red vest and controls the Bey's Fire moves.

BLADER QUOTE

"A silent flame and some freezing ice. Together the two of us are not so nice!"

KUMASUKE
BEYBLADE: ROCK ORSO

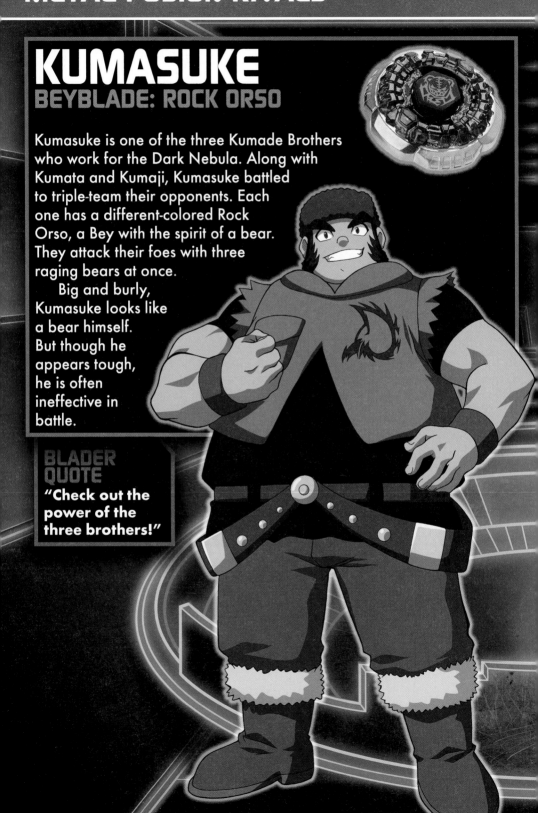

Kumasuke is one of the three Kumade Brothers who work for the Dark Nebula. Along with Kumata and Kumaji, Kumasuke battled to triple-team their opponents. Each one has a different-colored Rock Orso, a Bey with the spirit of a bear. They attack their foes with three raging bears at once.

Big and burly, Kumasuke looks like a bear himself. But though he appears tough, he is often ineffective in battle.

BLADER QUOTE

"Check out the power of the three brothers!"

TERU

BEYBLADE: EARTH VIRGO

Once a professional ballet dancer, Teru had an accident onstage that left him recovering in a hospital bed for months. Watching Gingka on TV inspired him to become a Blader. He battles with Earth Virgo, a Bey with the grace of a ballerina. Teru calls Earth Virgo "my beloved prima donna."

BLADER QUOTE
"All right, let's dance!"

SORA

BEYBLADE: CYBER PEGASUS

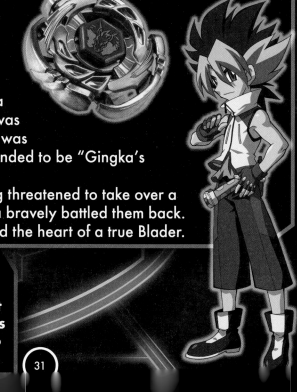

When Sora interrupted Kenta in the middle of a battle, he was loud-mouthed and cocky. He was such a big fan, he even pretended to be "Gingka's number-one apprentice."

But when Busujima's gang threatened to take over a stadium in a small town, Sora bravely battled them back. That's when he proved he had the heart of a true Blader.

BLADER QUOTE
"Beyblade is all about a Blader's spirit. I won't give in to a guy who has no respect for that, who thinks it's a joke."

BUSUJIMA
BEYBLADE: ROCK SCORPIO

Busujima leads a gang of Bladers who took over a Beystadium in a small town. Busujima greased the floor of the stadium with oil so that his opponents' Beys couldn't spin properly, while his Rock Scorpio's spiked bottom gave it traction to keep spinning.

The first time Busujima faced Sora, Busujima's followers helped their leader cheat. The second time, Kenta battled all the gang members at once while Sora and Busujima went one-on-one. Then Gingka swooped in to make sure that Busujima and his gang left town — for good.

DID YOU KNOW?

The spikes in Busujima's hair and on his jacket resemble the sharp, pointed stinger of a scorpion.

BLADER QUOTE
"No one cares how you win, as long as you win."

METAL FUSION BEYS

"Beys aren't to blame for their behavior. Whether they're used for good or used for bad is up to the Blader." — Madoka

Every Blader takes his Bey into battle with him. Each Bey has a spirit inside it, and that form is revealed on the battlefield. There are four main types of Beys: Beys with strong Attack power; Beys with strong Defense; Beys with Stamina that allows them to keep spinning for a long time; and Beys with a balance of all three traits.

In the pages that follow, you'll learn about the Beys from the Metal Fusion TV series, and you'll also get info you need when choosing your own Beys to battle with.

STORM PEGASUS 105RF
BB-28
TYPE: ATTACK

	ATTACK	DEFENSE	STAMINA
ENERGY RING™: PEGASUS	★ ★ ★ ★	★ ★	★
FUSION WHEEL™: STORM	★ ★ ★ ★	★	★
SPIN TRACK™: 105 LOW-PROFILE TRACK.	★		
PERFORMANCE TIP™: RF RUBBER FLAT GENERATES AN AGGRESSIVE SPIN.	★ ★ ★ ★ ★ ★	★	

ON THE SHOW
BLADER: GINGKA
SPECIAL MOVES:
Pegasus Starblast Attack, Pegasus Tornado Wing, Meteor Shower Attack, Pegasus Storm Bringer, Pegasus Galaxy Nova

Pegasus was the first Bey created from the meteorite that hit Koma village. Gingka got Pegasus from his father, Ryo, and the Blader and his new Bey developed a strong and rare bond. "No matter who I battle, as long I've got my Pegasus I like my chances," Gingka has said.

DID YOU KNOW?
Gingka used Storm Pegasus during his final battle with Ryuga. Gingka and Pegasus won the battle, but when it was over, Pegasus evaporated into glittering dust and flew up into the sky.

Want to know more about what the stats for each Bey mean? Turn to the Blader's Battle Guide at the end of this book.

LIGHTNING L-DRAGO 100HF
BB-43
TYPE: ATTACK

	ATTACK	DEFENSE	STAMINA
ENERGY RING™: L-DRAGO	★ ★ ★ ★ ★	★ ★	
FUSION WHEEL™: LIGHTNING	★ ★ ★ ★ ★ ★	⊥	⊥
SPIN TRACK™: 100 LOW-PROFILE TRACK.	★ ★		
PERFORMANCE TIP™: HF HOLE FLAT TIP FOR A STEADY ATTACK.	★ ★ ★ ★		★ ★ ★

ON THE SHOW
BLADER: RYUGA
SPECIAL MOVES:
Dragon Emperor Soaring Bite Strike, Dragon Emperor Soaring Destruction

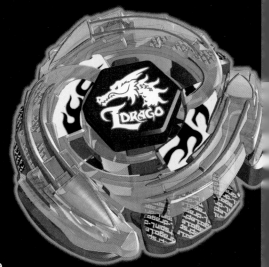

Known as "The Forbidden Bey," L-Drago was created from a meteorite carrying dark energy from the far regions of space. This Bey feeds on negative emotions, such as fear and anger. Every time it defeats another Bey in battle, it gets stronger and more powerful.

DID YOU KNOW?
While most Beys rotate to the right and circle to the left, L-Drago does the opposite. It rotates to the left in a counterclockwise direction. That gives it an advantage. Instead of chasing its opponent around the stadium, it can swoop in from the opposite direction to attack.

ROCK LEONE 145WB

BB-30
TYPE: DEFENSE

	ATTACK	DEFENSE	STAMINA
ENERGY RING™: LEONE	★	★ ★ ★ ★	★ ★
FUSION WHEEL™: ROCK	★	★ ★ ★ ★	★ ★
SPIN TRACK™: 145 HIGH-PROFILE TRACK.			★ ★
PERFORMANCE TIP™: WB WIDE BALL FOR ULTIMATE STABILITY.	★	★ ★ ★ ★ ★	★

ON THE SHOW

BLADER: KYOYA

SPECIAL MOVES: Lion Gale-Force Wall, Lion 100 Fang Fury, Lion Wild Wind Fang Dance, King Lion Tearing Blast, King Lion Furious Blast Shot

When Kyoya cries, "Roar, Leone!" this Bey spins so fast it swirls up the surrounding wind, creating an invisible wall around it. That makes Leone a strong Defense-type Bey. "Kyoya's Leone is like a wild animal enjoying the hunt," Kenta has said. When Leone really gets spinning, it can become super destructive.

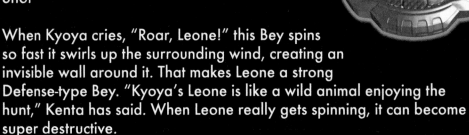

DARK WOLF DF145FS

BB-29
TYPE: BALANCE

	ATTACK	DEFENSE	STAMINA
ENERGY RING™: WOLF	★ ★ ★	★ ★	★ ★
FUSION WHEEL™: DARK	★ ★ ★	★ ★ ★	★ ★
SPIN TRACK™: DF145 DOWN FORCE HARD-HITTING BLADES.		★	★ ★
PERFORMANCE TIP™: FS FLAT SPIKE CONTROLS PACE.	★ ★ ★	★	★ ★ ★

DARK BULL H145SD
BB-40
TYPE: BALANCE

	ATTACK	DEFENSE	STAMINA
ENERGY RING™: BULL	★ ★ ★	★ ★ ★	★
FUSION WHEEL™: DARK	★ ★ ★	★ ★ ★	★ ★
SPIN TRACK™: 145 DOUBLE HORNS GRAB OPPONENTS.		★ ★ ★	★
PERFORMANCE TIP™: SD SEMI-DEFENSE STEADIES TRAJECTORY.	★	★ ★ ★	★ ★ ★

ON THE SHOW
BLADER: BENKEI
SPECIAL MOVES: Bull Uppercut, Dark Bull Red-Horn Uppercut, Tornado Bull Uppercut, Dark Bull Maximum Stampede

This ferocious, rampaging bovine was given to Benkei by Doji, who hoped that Dark Bull could defeat Gingka's Pegasus. It couldn't, but Benkei and Dark Bull went on to win many battles after that.

ON THE SHOW
BLADER: DOJI
SPECIAL MOVE: Darkness Howling Blazer

Doji usually gets other Bladers to do his dirty work for him, but when he does battle, he uses Dark Wolf. Considered by some to be the ultimate Balance-type, this Bey has no weak points for an opponent to take advantage of. But it lacks the strong attacks of some other types — like Gingka's Pegasus.

METAL FUSION BEYS

FLAME SAGITTARIO C145S
BB-35
TYPE: STAMINA

	ATTACK	DEFENSE	STAMINA
ENERGY RING™: SAGITTARIO	★	★ ★	★ ★ ★ ★
FUSION WHEEL™: FLAME	★	★ ★	★ ★ ★ ★
SPIN TRACK™: C145 WHIPPING CLAWS STRIKE OPPONENTS.		★ ★	★ ★
PERFORMANCE TIP™: S SPIKE TIP MAINTAINS STAMINA.	★	★ ★	★ ★ ★ ★

ON THE SHOW
BLADER: KENTA
SPECIAL MOVE: Sagittario Flame Claw

Kenta's Sagittario boasts some very strong Stamina moves. When Kenta first battled Gingka, even Pegasus's strongest attacks couldn't bring it down right away. Hit it hard, and Sagittario just keeps going.

DARK GASHER CH120FS
BB-31
TYPE: BALANCE

	ATTACK	DEFENSE	STAMINA
ENERGY RING™: GASHER	★ ★ ★	★ ★ ★	★
FUSION WHEEL™: DARK	★ ★ ★	★ ★ ★	★ ★
SPIN TRACK™: CH120 CHANGE HEIGHT FOR OPTIMUM ATTACK POSITION.			★ ★
PERFORMANCE TIP™: FS FLAT SPIKE CONTROLS THE SPIN.	★ ★ ★	★	★ ★ ★

EARTH EAGLE 145WD

BB-47
TYPE: BALANCE

	ATTACK	DEFENSE	STAMINA
ENERGY RING™: EAGLE	★★	★	★★★★
FUSION WHEEL™: EARTH	★	★	★★★★★
SPIN TRACK™: 145 HIGH-PROFILE TRACK.			★★
PERFORMANCE TIP™: WD WIDE DEFENSE TIP FOR ENDURANCE.		★★★★★	★★★

ON THE SHOW
BLADER: TSUBASA
SPECIAL MOVES: Metal-Wing Smash, Counter Stance, Diving Crush, Stream Slash Attack, Counter Smash

When Eagle attacks, it comes at an opponent from all sides. Many of its special moves, such as Metal-Wing Smash and Diving Crush, involve the Bey soaring above the stadium and then smashing down on its opponent. With Counter Stance, Eagle creates a shock wave that allows it to soar on any wind, like an eagle in flight.

ON THE SHOW
BLADER: TETSUYA
SPECIAL MOVE: Six Crab Shake

When Tetsuya wanted to join Dark Nebula, he allowed Doji to experiment on Mad Gasher. Doji transformed the crablike Bey into Dark Gasher, a more powerful Bey with a twelve-bladed Fusion Wheel. With its new move, Six Crab Shake, Gasher strikes out at its opponents with its blades the way a real crab pinches with its claws.

FLAME LIBRA T125ES
BB-48
TYPE: STAMINA

	ATTACK	DEFENSE	STAMINA
ENERGY RING™: LIBRA	★ ★	★	★ ★ ★ ★
FUSION WHEEL™: FLAME	★	★ ★	★ ★ ★ ★
SPIN TRACK™: T125 TORNADO CREATES SUSTAINING VORTEX.		★	
PERFORMANCE TIP™: ES ETERNAL SPIKE TIP MAXIMIZES STAMINA.		★ ★	★ ★ ★ ★ ★

ON THE SHOW
BLADER: YU
SPECIAL MOVES: Sonic Buster, Libra Inferno Blast, Sonic Shield, Sonic Wave

Yu's Flame Libra is best known for its devastating attacks using sonic waves. These vibrations shoot all the way to the sky and leave huge craters in their wake. With Inferno Blast, Libra creates supersonic waves that capture other Beys even as they protect Libra like heavy armor.

BURN FIREBLAZE 135MS
BB-59
TYPE: STAMINA

	ATTACK	DEFENSE	STAMINA
ENERGY RING™: FIREBLAZE	★	★	★ ★ ★ ★ ★
FUSION WHEEL™: BURN	★	★ ★	★ ★ ★ ★
SPIN TRACK™: 135 MID-PROFILE TRACK.			★
PERFORMANCE TIP™: MS METAL SPIKE TIP INCREASES DURABILITY AND STAMINA.		★	★ ★ ★ ★ ★ ★

STORM AQUARIO 100HF/S
BB-37
TYPE: ATTACK

	ATTACK	DEFENSE	STAMINA
ENERGY RING™: AQUARIO	★ ★ ★ ★	★	★ ★
FUSION WHEEL™: STORM	★ ★ ★ ★	★	★
SPIN TRACK™: 100 LOW-PROFILE TRACK.	★ ★		
PERFORMANCE TIP™: HF/S CONVERT TIP FROM HOLE FLAT TO SPIKE TO CHANGE PERFORMANCE.	★ ★ ★ ★		★ ★ ★

ON THE SHOW
BLADER: HIKARU
SPECIAL MOVE: Aquario Infinite Assault

When Aquario hits the stadium, it washes over its opponents like a tidal wave. With Aquario Infinite Assault, the Bey circles its opponent so fast that it appears to multiply. Then it strikes like a powerful wave.

ON THE SHOW
BLADER: PHOENIX
SPECIAL MOVE: Burning Firestrike

Burn Fireblaze's metal performance tip creates a lot of friction and resistance, giving it extra power. When Fireblaze uses Burning Firestrike, it causes a huge explosion on impact.

EVIL GEMIOS DF145FS
BB-56
TYPE: BALANCE

	ATTACK	DEFENSE	STAMINA
ENERGY RING™: GEMIOS	★ ★ ★	★ ★ ★	★
FUSION WHEEL™: EVIL	★ ★ ★	★ ★ ★	★
SPIN TRACK™: DF145 DOWN FORCE HARD-HITTING BLADES.		★	★ ★
PERFORMANCE TIP™: FS FLAT SPIKE CONTROLS PACE.	★ ★ ★	★	★ ★ ★

ON THE SHOW
BLADERS: DAN AND REIKI
SPECIAL MOVES: Gemios Downburst, Blaze Wall, Icicle Attack

Dan and Reiki's Bey is a combination of two powers: Fire and Ice. Blaze Wall is its fiery attack, while Icicle Attack freezes opponents. When it performs Gemios Downburst, the two powers combine, and twin fire and ice tornadoes swirl across the stadium.

THERMAL PISCES T125ES
BB-57
TYPE: STAMINA

	ATTACK	DEFENSE	STAMINA
ENERGY RING™: PISCES	★ ★	★	★ ★ ★ ★
FUSION WHEEL™: THERMAL	★ ★	★	★ ★ ★ ★
SPIN TRACK™: T125 TORNADO CREATES SUSTAINING VORTEX.		★	
PERFORMANCE TIP™: ES ETERNAL SPIKE TIP MAXIMIZES		★ ★	★ ★ ★ ★ ★

EARTH VIRGO GB145BS
BB-60
TYPE: STAMINA

	ATTACK	DEFENSE	STAMINA
ENERGY RING™: VIRGO	★	★ ★	★ ★ ★ ★
FUSION WHEEL™: EARTH	★	★	★ ★ ★ ★ ★
SPIN TRACK™: GB145 GRAVITY BALL INCREASES STAMINA AND STABILITY.	★ ★	★ ★	★ ★ ★
PERFORMANCE TIP™: BS BOTTOM SPIKE MAINTAINS SPIN.	★ ★ ★ ★	★ ★ ★	★ ★ ★ ★

ON THE SHOW
BLADER: TERU

Like a prima ballerina, this Bey has perfect balance. It can spin and spin without wobbling. It owes its balance to two metal balls inside its Spin Track. Its move, Pirouette Tour, allows it to spin with amazing speed.

ON THE SHOW
BLADER: RYUTARO
SPECIAL MOVE: Distortion Drive

Thermal Pisces seems to float in the air, and when Ryutaro uses his Distortion Drive move, his opponents get woozy and see illusions. That's because when Pisces spins, it changes the airflow around it, making things look distorted.

POISON SERPENT SW145SD
BB-69
TYPE: BALANCE

	ATTACK	DEFENSE	STAMINA
ENERGY RING™: SERPENT	★ ★ ★	★ ★ ★	★
FUSION WHEEL™: POISON	★ ★ ★	★ ★ ★	★
SPIN TRACK™: SW145 SWITCH IT FROM ATTACK TO DEFENSE.	★	★ ★ ★	★ ★
PERFORMANCE TIP™: SD SEMI-DEFENSE STEADIES TRAJECTORY.	★	★ ★ ★	★ ★ ★

ON THE SHOW
BLADER: REIJI
SPECIAL MOVE: Venom Strike

Reiji's Bey has fifteen blades on its Spin Track, but they don't seem all that powerful. But those blades slowly chip away at an opponent's Bey, gradually weakening it — the way a snake's poison slowly weakens its prey. Then, when its opponent slows down, Poison Serpent moves in to finish the fight.

ROCK SCORPIO T125JB
BB-65
TYPE: DEFENSE

	ATTACK	DEFENSE	STAMINA
ENERGY RING™: SCORPIO	★ ★	★ ★ ★ ★	★
FUSION WHEEL™: ROCK	★	★ ★ ★ ★	★ ★
SPIN TRACK™: T125 TORNADO CREATES SUSTAINING VORTEX.		★	
PERFORMANCE TIP™: JB JOG BALL TIP GRIPS SURFACES FOR MORE STABILITY AND ENDURANCE.	★ ★	★ ★ ★ ★ ★	★ ★

ROCK ORSO D125B
BB-51
TYPE: DEFENSE

	ATTACK	DEFENSE	STAMINA
ENERGY RING™: ORSO	★ ★	★ ★ ★	★ ★
FUSION WHEEL™: ROCK	★	★ ★ ★ ★	★ ★
SPIN TRACK™: D125 A BROAD DEFENSE RIDGE.	★ ★	★ ★	★
PERFORMANCE TIP™: B BALL TIP KEEPS TOP STEADY.	★ ★ ★ ★	★ ★ ★ ★	★ ★ ★

ON THE SHOW
BLADER: KUMASUKE

SPECIAL MOVES: Bear Claw Slash, Triple Orso Step

Imagine facing a big, strong bear in the stadium — that's what it's like to battle Rock Orso. This Bey has very high Defense stats and a Performance Tip that keeps it spinning even when it gets hit hard. Its strongest attack move is Bear Claw Smash.

ON THE SHOW
BLADER: BUSUJIMA

Rock Scorpio's spike-covered performance tip gives it extra stability on a slick surface. Busujima uses this special feature to cheat. He pours oil on the stadium floor so opponents slip while Rock Scorpio stays steady.

GINGKA VS. ONE HUNDRED FACE HUNTERS

When Gingka first appeared, Kyoya ordered Benkei and ninety-nine other Face Hunters to battle Gingka all at once. For most Bladers, this would spell the end, but Gingka defeated every last one of them.

FLAME LIBRA DEFEATS PEGASUS

Many Bladers competed in the Survival Battle challenge, but the final battle came down to two: Gingka and Yu. Innocent-looking Yu didn't appear to be much of a threat, but he stunned everyone when his Flame Libra took down Pegasus with a supersonic move: Libra Inferno Blast.

SIX-BLADER BATTLE ROYAL

In a special Battle Blader Challenge match, six top competitors faced off to win ten thousand Bey Points. Gingka, Kyoya, Tsubasa, Yu, Kenta, and Hyoma all entered the battle royal. Tsubasa eliminated Hyoma, and then Gingka took down Yu and Tsubasa — and himself in the process. That made room for Kyoya to defeat Kenta for the victory — and all the points.

YU STAYS STRONG

As punishment for losing a match, Doji made Yu battle Reiji and his Poison Serpent. Flame Libra grew weaker and weaker during the match, and Yu realized that Gingka was right — the Dark Nebula is an evil organization, and he shouldn't have joined. That knowledge gave him the strength to fuel one last sonic move from Libra, helping Yu break free.

BEST FRIENDS BATTLE

Benkei has always looked up to Kyoya, his best friend. Then they're pitted against each other in a Battle Bladers challenge match. Benkei's Dark Bull developed a new move during the fight, but Leone's King Lion Tearing Blast finished him. "You're stronger than you were," Kyoya told Benkei. "But you'd better get even stronger for your next battle."

THE FINAL BATTLE

The last Battle Bladers match was about more than proving who was number one. L-Drago's power was so strong that the Bey was poised to destroy the whole world. Pegasus and L-Drago took their battle high into the stratosphere. Then Gingka called on the combined power of all Bladers everywhere, giving Pegasus the strength it needed to destroy L-Drago and save the world.

THIS IS IT!

If you thought the Battle Bladers tournament was exciting, then hold on to your launcher! In Metal Masters, there's a new competition, and this one is bigger than ever: **The Beyblade World Championship.**

Once word got around that Gingka won Battle Bladers, Bladers from all over the world wanted the chance the defeat him and earn the title of number-one Blader. So the WBBA, now headed by Ryo, created a global competition.

In the Beyblade World Championship, Bladers from different countries compete to represent their nation. The final teams will travel around the globe, competing against new Beys, meeting new friends, and learning new tricks and strategies.

In this high-spirited competition, only the best of the best will compete. Some will win, some will lose . . . others will face challenges that will test everything they know about the world of Beyblade.

METAL MASTERS BLADERS

Before the Beyblade World Championships can begin, Bladers from each country or continent have to compete to see who will represent them. Many will battle, but only the very best can represent their nation.

Each team can consist of five members: three regular members, one substitute, and one technical support member. They will face one another in a series of battles in every land to determine which nation's team is the best . . . and decide, once and for all, the number-one Blader in the world.

BLADER QUOTE

"I will take everyone's spirit with me into the world. I will burn with all the fire I've got!"

GINGKA
BEYBLADE: GALAXY PEGASUS

Gingka might be the world's number-one Blader, but it's hard to celebrate because he misses Pegasus. Then his dad sends him into the mountains of Koma Village where he finds a Legendary Bey . . . Galaxy Pegasus.

With his new Bey by his side, Gingka is ready to lead the team from Japan, Gangan Galaxy, on their quest to be the world's best. But first he has to figure out how to control the awesome power of Galaxy Pegasus.

DID YOU KNOW? Gingka's flowing white scarf resembles the white wings of his Pegasus.

MASAMUNE
BEYBLADE: RAY STRIKER

Masamune was out of the country during the Battle Bladers tournament, and he came back to Japan like a whirlwind. He's angry because he missed his chance to prove he's the number-one Blader, and he calls Gingka "a goofy, scarf-wearing guy."

As you can imagine, Masamune gets on Gingka's nerves. He challenges Gingka to battle after battle, losing every time. Then, when he finally wins, he insists that makes him the new number one! He's super competitive and won't rest until the whole world knows he's the best.

DID YOU KNOW? In China, Masamune really, really wants to see a panda and is disappointed when there are none in sight. He's bummed about the country's "serious lack of pandas."

TSUBASA
BEYBLADE: EARTH EAGLE

Tsubasa is one of the regular members of Team Gangan Galaxy. During the qualifying matches, he felt a dark power come over him as he battled Kyoya. That power almost destroyed Earth Eagle and Rock Leone, but Eagle saved them all with a burst of pure light.

After the battle, Tsubasa wonders what happened to him. He's worried. But surely he can resist anything with Eagle at his side . . . or can he?

YU

BEYBLADE: FLAME LIBRA

Yu has joined forces with Gingka and his friends, and now he's determined to get a spot on Team Gangan Galaxy. He learns new moves with his Flame Libra. But he loses his chance when he's defeated by a newcomer named Masamune.

Then Yu gets lucky: When Kyoya decides not to be on the team, he and Tsubasa battle for the open spot. Yu tries to bring down Tsubasa's Eagle with a sonic attack that fills the sky with rainbow light. But in the end, Eagle is victorious.

That leaves Yu as the team's official substitute, and he's not happy. He's sure he'll never get a chance to battle. But in a competition like this, you never know what might happen. . . .

DID YOU KNOW? When Yu reaches for a snack — which is pretty often — he usually chooses ice cream.

BLADER QUOTE

"It's all good. All that matters is ... we're a team!"

MADOKA

Madoka has a new job — she's the top mechanic for the WBBA. She's also the technical support member of Team Gangan Galaxy. Madoka will travel with the team, keeping their Beys in good condition and offering strategy and advice, as she always does.

"Is that all you've got? This is my first battle in a long time, so could you try to make it more fun?"

RYUGA

BEYBLADE: METEO L-DRAGO

Ryuga's back! He trained very hard to get rid of the dark energy inside him, and now he has become one with the power of the cosmos contained in his Bey.

Ryuga's new Bey is Meteo L-Drago. He's anxious to see how his Bey will perform in a match against Gingka's Galaxy Pegasus. The last time L-Drago and Pegasus faced off, the match nearly destroyed the world. What will happen this time?

JAPAN
TEAM GANGAN GALAXY

Because he was the Battle Bladers champion, Gingka automatically earned a spot on Team Gangan Galaxy. After a series of qualifying matches, Masamune and Tsubasa took the next two spots. Yu is the team substitute, and Madoka is their technical support member.

Madoka is good at keeping the team in line. Tsubasa is always lost in thought. Yu is easily distracted, and Gingka and Masamune don't get along. Madoka keeps them focused on their goals. All in all, Japan is a strong team with some of the best fighting spirit in the competition.

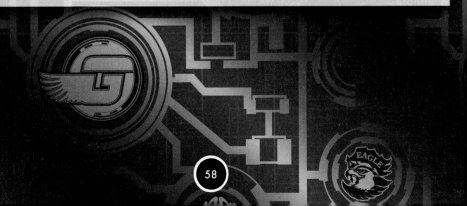

YU

MADOKA

TSUBASA

MASAMUNE

GINGKA

TEAM WANG HU ZHONG

This team takes their training very seriously. Bladers learn the art of Beyblade at a martial-arts facility high on a mountaintop. Dashan is a super disciplined Blader who acts as team leader. His teammate Chiyun is a young boy, but he's got the skills of an expert. And substitute Mei-Mei is cute, but few Bladers can defeat her in a battle.

Then there's Chaoxin. This flashy Blader is in the game for the glory of his fans. Girls everywhere adore him. But does he have the skills to back up his image?

MEI-MEI

DASHAN

CHAOXIN

CHIYUN

EUROPE

TEAM EXCALIBUR

The leader of this team, Julian, is an expert equestrian who battles with Gravity Destroyer, a Bey with a warrior spirit. Julian is very confident in his abilities, and in one match he boldly challenges three Bladers to fight against him.

Also on Team Excalibur is Klaus, a strong Blader who won't back down when things get tough. Then there are Sophie and Wales, two Bladers Julian calls his "Twin Jewels." They often team up to battle together, and they claim they've never been defeated.

KLAUS

JULIAN

SOPHIE

WALES

AFRICA

TEAM WILD FANG

That's right — Kyoya is on Team Wild Fang! So why did he refuse to join Team Gangan Galaxy? It's because Kyoya wants to defeat one person and one person only: Gingka. Joining Africa's team will ensure he'll get a chance to face Gingka again.

Then there's the rest of the team. They're good friends and loyal to one another. Nile has some serious skills. Damoure isn't as confident as he could be, but his eyesight is amazing, and helps him to calculate his opponent's next move. Then there's the Masked Bull, who battles with a Dark Bull. If he looks familiar, it's because he's an old friend — Benkei!

DAMOURE

KYOYA

NILE

THE MASKED BULL

BRAZIL

TEAM GARCIA

For Team Brazil, Blading is a family activity. The team is made up of the four Garcia siblings: Argo, Selen, Ian, and Enso, the team sub. They grew up learning to Blade together against tough competitors on the streets of Brazil.

Selen and Enso often battle together, and both use a Ray Gasher. But Argo and Ian use Beys that Gingka and his team have never seen before: Ray Gill and Cyclone Herculeo.

USA

TEAM STAR BREAKER

The members of Team Star Breaker are all fierce competitors who take pleasure in decimating their opponents. They can be cruel and heartless in battle, and it seems like they'll do anything to win.

So what's up with this team? The answer lies with their mysterious owner, Dr. Ziggurat. He runs HD Academy, where Bladers use state-of-the-art equipment to train. Gingka and his friends suspect that there's something odd going on there . . . but when they discover what it is, it might already be too late.

DAMIAN

ZEO

JACK

METAL MASTERS BEYS

In any Beyblade battle, knowing about your opponent's Bey always gives you an advantage. It's the best way to develop a strategy in battle.

But in the Beyblade World Championship tournament, Gingka and Team Gangan Galaxy will face Beys that they've never seen before — Beys with amazing moves. They'll have to use all their skills to figure out how to defeat these new opponents.

GALAXY PEGASUS W105R2F
BB-70
TYPE: ATTACK

	ATTACK	DEFENSE	STAMINA
ENERGY RING™: PEGASUS II	★ ★ ★ ★ ★	★	★
FUSION WHEEL™: GALAXY	★ ★ ★ ★ ★ ★	★	
SPIN TRACK™: W105 WINGS PUSH DOWN TO STABILIZE THE SPINNING ATTACK.	★	★	
PERFORMANCE TIP™: R2F RIGHT RUBBER FLAT FOR INCREASED GRIPPING POWER.	★ ★ ★ ★ ★ ★	★	

ON THE SHOW

BLADER: GINGKA
Special Move:
Star Booster Attack

The villagers of Koma Village created Galaxy Pegasus, a Bey so powerful they believed no one could control it. So they sealed it away. But Ryo, Gingka's father, sent Gingka to find this Legendary Bey. When Gingka reached out to touch it, a bright light burst forth, and when it died down, Gingka was holding Galaxy Pegasus in his hand.

Galaxy Pegasus has more power than Gingka has ever seen. But unless he can learn to control it, he won't be able to succeed in battle.

RAY STRIKER D125CS
BB-71
TYPE: ATTACK

	ATTACK	DEFENSE	STAMINA
ENERGY RING™: STRIKER	★ ★ ★ ★	★ ★	★
FUSION WHEEL™: RAY	★ ★ ★ ★	★	★ ★
SPIN TRACK™: D125 A BROAD DEFENSE RIDGE.		★ ★	★
PERFORMANCE TIP™: CS COATING SPIKE STEADIES TOP AND PROVIDES QUICK MOVEMENT.	★ ★ ★ ★		★ ★ ★

ON THE SHOW

BLADER: MASAMUNE
Special Move: Lightning Sword Flash

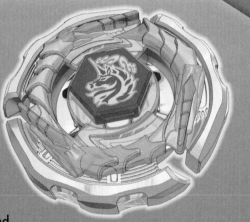

The spirit form of Masamune's Ray Striker — a unicorn that is bathed in green light — is often revealed in battle. When Ray Striker performs Lightning Sword Flash for Masamune, purple lightning shoots from its horn.

　　Masamune's connection to Ray Striker is very strong. "The Blader and the Bey have to be a team," he says. "Striker and I work together with one heart and mind. Our power is unlimited. We won't lose to anybody."

METEO L-DRAGO LWIO5LF
BB-88
TYPE: ATTACK

	ATTACK	DEFENSE	STAMINA
ENERGY RING™: L-DRAGO II	★ ★ ★ ★	★	★ ★ ★ ★
FUSION WHEEL™: METEO	★ ★ ★ ★ ★	★ ★	★
SPIN TRACK™: LW105 LEFT WINGS HELP STABILIZE LEFT-SPIN ATTACKS WITH A DOWNWARD THRUST.	★	★	
PERFORMANCE TIP™: LF LEFT FLAT TIP INCREASES SURFACE AREA AND GRIPPING POWER.	★ ★ ★ ★ ★ ★	★	

ON THE SHOW

BLADER: RYUGA
Special Move: Dragon Emperor Supreme Flight

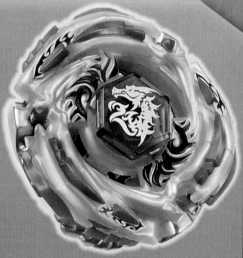

While Lightning L-Drago took the form of a purple dragon pulsing with dark energy, Meteo L-Drago burns with red fire and the energy of the universe. Meteo L-Drago is an Attack-type, but it can withstand punishment from the strongest Beys. Ryuga has a connection with his Bey that rivals Gingka's connection to Pegasus.

DID YOU KNOW?
Like many Beys, L-Drago is named after a constellation in the sky: Draco, which is shaped like a dragon.

ROCK ZURAFA R145WB
BB-78
TYPE: DEFENSE

	ATTACK	DEFENSE	STAMINA
ENERGY RING™: ZURAFA	★	★ ★ ★ ★ ★	★
FUSION WHEEL™: ROCK	★	★ ★ ★ ★	★ ★
SPIN TRACK™: R145 RUBBER SHOCK ABSORBER FOR POWERFUL DEFENSE.		★ ★ ★	★ ★
PERFORMANCE TIP™: WB WIDE BALL FOR AWESOME STABILITY.	★	★ ★ ★ ★ ★	★

ON THE SHOW

BLADER: DASHAN FROM TEAM WANG HU ZHONG
Special Moves: Storm Surge, Crushing Blast

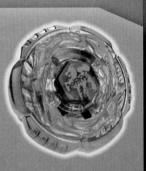

This Defense-type Bey boasts many moves, a reflection of all the training Dashan has done. Rock Zurafa can withstand lots of attacks without getting damaged, thanks to the rubber wings on its Spin Track. The spirit inside it is a Qilin, a mythical Chinese creature that resembles a giraffe.

GRAVITY DESTROYER AD145WD
BB-80
TYPE: DEFENSE

	ATTACK	DEFENSE	STAMINA
ENERGY RING™: DESTROYER	★ ★	★ ★ ★ ★ ★	
FUSION WHEEL™: GRAVITY	★ ★	★ ★ ★ ★ ★	
SPIN TRACK™: AD145 ARMOR DEFENSE CREATES A STRONG, SOLID BASE THAT CAN WITHSTAND HITS.		★	★ ★
PERFORMANCE TIP™: WD WIDE DEFENSE TIP FOR ENDURANCE.		★ ★ ★ ★	★ ★

THERMAL LACERTA WA130HF
BB-74
TYPE: BALANCE

	ATTACK	DEFENSE	STAMINA
ENERGY RING™: LACERTA	★ ★ ★	★ ★	★ ★
FUSION WHEEL™: THERMAL	★ ★	★	★ ★ ★ ★
SPIN TRACK™: WA130 WING ATTACK ABSORBS HITS & STRIKES OPPONENTS.		★ ★	
PERFORMANCE TIP™: HF HOLE FLAT TIP FOR A STEADY ATTACK.	★ ★ ★ ★		★ ★ ★

ON THE SHOW

BLADER: CHIYUN, TEAM WANG HU ZHONG
Special Moves: Tempestuous Whirlwind Sword

Thermal Lacerta is a Balance-type Bey with a variety of useful moves. It owes its balance to its thick Fusion Wheel, which gives the Bey extra defensive strength as well as stability.

The spirit of Lacerta resembles a big lizardlike monster, like the kind you might see in a movie. Like those movie monsters, Lacerta can really knock down its opponents.

ON THE SHOW

BLADER: JULIAN, TEAM EXCALIBUR
Special Move: Black Excalibur

Gravity Destroyer has an extra-wide performance tip that helps keep this Bey spinning, no matter how hard it gets hit. Gravity Destroyer can take attack after attack without wobbling, just like a knight in heavy armor.

When Julian's Gravity Destroyer attacks, it looks like a knight carrying a sword. This Bey has one thing in common with L-Drago: It can rotate to the left.

GRAND CETUS (BLUE) WD145RS
BB-82A
TYPE: DEFENSE

	ATTACK	DEFENSE	STAMINA
ENERGY RING™: CETUS	★ ★	★ ★ ★ ★	★
FUSION WHEEL™: GRAND	★ ★	★ ★ ★ ★	★
SPIN TRACK™: WD145 WIDE DEFENSE RIDGES TO BLOCK ATTACKS.		★ ★ ★	★ ★
PERFORMANCE TIP™: RS RUBBER SPIKE HELPS TOP STAY IN PLACE AND SPIN LONGER.	★	★ ★ ★ ★ ★	★

ON THE SHOW

BLADER: WALES, TEAM EXCALIBUR
Special Moves: Grand Fleet, Grand Deucalion

In the night sky, the constellation Cetus is named after a giant whale. So it's no surprise that Grand Cetus uses special moves that involve water. When Wales uses Grand Fleet, his blue Cetus takes the form of a blue whale. All the Beys in the stadium are sucked into the powerful swirling waters.

GRAND CAPRICORN 145D
B-134
TYPE: DEFENSE

	ATTACK	DEFENSE	STAMINA
ENERGY RING™: CAPRICORN	★ ★ ★ ★	★ ★	★
FUSION WHEEL™: GRAND	★ ★	★ ★ ★ ★	★
SPIN TRACK™: 145 HIGH-PROFILE TRACK.			★ ★
PERFORMANCE TIP™: D TOUGH DEFENSE TIP CAN WITHSTAND ATTACKS.	★	★ ★ ★ ★	★ ★

GRAND CETUS (WHITE) T125RS
B-82B
TYPE: DEFENSE

	ATTACK	DEFENSE	STAMINA
ENERGY RING™: CETUS	★ ★	★ ★ ★ ★	★
FUSION WHEEL™: GRAND	★ ★	★ ★ ★ ★	★
SPIN TRACK™: T125 TORNADO CREATES SUSTAINING VORTEX.		★	
PERFORMANCE TIP™: RS RUBBER SPIKE HELPS TOP STAY IN PLACE AND SPIN LONGER.	★	★ ★ ★ ★ ★	★

ON THE SHOW

BLADER: SOPHIE, TEAM EXCALIBUR
Special Moves: Grand Maelstrom, Grand Victorie, Grand Deucalion

Sophie's white Cetus takes the form of a white whale when she uses Grand Victorie. It makes a powerful impact. But she and Wales get their best results from a combined move, Grand Deucalion, which creates a virtual tsunami. The massive wave of energy can take down just about any opponent.

ON THE SHOW

BLADER: KLAUS, TEAM EXCALIBUR
Special Moves: Claw of the Storm, First; Claw of the Storm, Second; Claw of the Storm, Third; Steel Darkness

Grand Capricorn can spin very quickly, sending other Beys flying. In battle, Klaus's Grand Capricorn can take a great deal of damage without faltering. Klaus's three Claw moves are attack moves, and each one is stronger than the last. These moves make Grand Capricorn tough to beat.

VULCAN HORUSEUS 145D
BB-P0I
TYPE: DEFENSE

	ATTACK	DEFENSE	STAMINA
ENERGY RING™: HORUSEUS	★ ★	★ ★ ★ ★	★
FUSION WHEEL™: VULCAN	★ ★	★ ★ ★ ★	★
SPIN TRACK™: 145 HIGH-PROFILE TRACK.			★ ★
PERFORMANCE TIP™: D TOUGH DEFENSE TIP CAN WITHSTAND ATTACKS.	★	★ ★ ★ ★	★ ★

▬ ON THE SHOW

BLADER: NILE, TEAM WILD FANG
Special Move: Mystic Zone

Nile's Vulcan Horuseus is one tough battler. It's known for its centrifugal force attacks, which are powered by a special glow that can spread from its Energy Ring to its Fusion Wheel. This Bey gets its name from the Egyptian god Horus, the falcon-headed god of the sky.

RAY GIL 100RSF
BB-9I
TYPE: ATTACK

	ATTACK	DEFENSE	STAMINA
ENERGY RING™: GIL	★ ★ ★ ★	★	★ ★
FUSION WHEEL™: RAY	★ ★ ★ ★	★	★ ★
SPIN TRACK™: 100 WINGS PUSH DOWN TO STABILIZE THE SPINNING ATTACK.	★ ★		
PERFORMANCE TIP™: RSF RUBBER SEMI-FLAT TIP GRIPS SURFACE FOR STRONG ATTACKS.	★ ★ ★ ★	★ ★	★

COUNTER SCORPIO 145D
B-125
TYPE: DEFENSE

	ATTACK	DEFENSE	STAMINA
ENERGY RING™: SCORPIO	★ ★	★ ★ ★ ★	★
FUSION WHEEL™: COUNTER	★	★ ★ ★ ★	★
SPIN TRACK™: 145 HIGH-PROFILE TRACK.			★ ★
PERFORMANCE TIP™: D TOUGH DEFENSE TIP CAN WITHSTAND ATTACKS.	★	★ ★ ★ ★	★ ★

ON THE SHOW

BLADER: DAMOURE, TEAM WILD FANG

This Bey gets its strong Defense power from its performance tip, which is wider than most. That gives Counter Scorpio more stability when it's hit by an opponent.

ON THE SHOW

BLADER: ARGO, TEAM GARCIA
Special Move: Keel Strangler

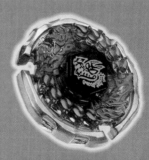

Argo hates to lose and, with Ray Gil at his side, it doesn't happen often. This Attack-type Bey is relentless in battle, delivering powerful blows to its opponents again and again.

CYCLONE HERCULEO 105F
BB-94
TYPE: ATTACK

	ATTACK	DEFENSE	STAMINA
ENERGY RING™: HERCULEO	★ ★ ★	★ ★	★ ★
FUSION WHEEL™: CYCLONE	★ ★ ★ ★ ★	★	★
SPIN TRACK™: 105 LOW-PROFILE TRACK.	★		
PERFORMANCE TIP™: F FLAT TIP FOR AGGRESSIVE MOVEMENT.	★ ★ ★ ★ ★	★	★

ON THE SHOW

BLADER: IAN, TEAM GARCIA
Special Move: Blazer Slash

Cyclone Herculeo is the only non-Ray Bey on Team Garcia. It gets its name from the Roman demi-god Hercules, who was known for his strength. And this Bey is unusually strong! It has five blades on its Fusion Wheel, giving it abnormally high attack power.

EVIL BEFALL UW145EWD
BB-100
TYPE: BALANCE

	ATTACK	DEFENSE	STAMINA
ENERGY RING™: BEFALL		★ ★	★ ★ ★ ★ ★
FUSION WHEEL™: EVIL	★ ★ ★	★ ★ ★	★
SPIN TRACK™: UW145 UPPER WING TRACK CHANGES FROM ATTACK TO DEFENSE.		★ ★	★ ★
PERFORMANCE TIP™: EWD ETERNAL WIDE DEFENSE TIP FOR AMAZING ENDURANCE.		★ ★ ★	★ ★ ★ ★ ★

HADES KERBECS BD145DS
BB-99
TYPE: STAMINA

	ATTACK	DEFENSE	STAMINA
ENERGY RING™: KERBECS	★ ★	★ ★	★ ★ ★
FUSION WHEEL™: HADES	★ ★ ★		★ ★ ★ ★
SPIN TRACK™: BD145 BOOST DISK WITH 2 MODES TO BOOST ATTACK OR STAMINA.	★	★ ★	★ ★
PERFORMANCE TIP™: DS DEFENSE SPIKE IS DESIGNED TO MAXIMIZE DEFENSE AND STAMINA.	★	★ ★ ★	★ ★ ★ ★

ON THE SHOW

BLADER: DAMIAN, TEAM STAR BREAKER
Special Moves: Hades Drive, Hades Gate

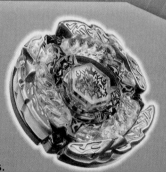

The spirit of this Bey is a three-headed dog resembling Cerberus, the beast with three heads that guards the Underworld in Greek mythology. Imagine a dog coming at you with three fierce jaws snapping, and you'll understand what it's like to be attacked by Hades Kerbecs.

ON THE SHOW

BLADER: JACK, TEAM STAR BREAKER
Special Moves: Befall the Ripper, Beautiful Dead

Jack's Bey takes the form of a peacock in battle, a fierce bird that shoots its feathers at opponents like arrows. Evil Befall has an extra-wide defensive performance tip that Jack says gives his Bey limitless Stamina.

FLAME BYXIS 230WD
BB-95
TYPE: BALANCE

	ATTACK	DEFENSE	STAMINA
ENERGY RING™: BYXIS	★ ★ ★	★	★ ★ ★
FUSION WHEEL™: FLAME	★	★ ★	★ ★ ★ ★
SPIN TRACK™: 230 AGGRESSIVE-HEIGHT PROFILE TO ATTACK FROM ABOVE.			★ ★
PERFORMANCE TIP™: WD WIDE DEFENSE TIP FOR ENDURANCE.		★ ★ ★ ★ ★	★ ★

ON THE SHOW

BLADER: ZEO, TEAM STAR BREAKER

Special Moves: Destiny Needle, Magnetic Needle Storm

When Madoka sees this Bey in action, she realizes that Flame Byxis can create magnetic fields of energy that throw its opponent off course. With Magnetic Needle Storm, Zeo's Bey generates a magnetic storm whose violent shock waves send other Beys flying.

TWISTED TEMPO 145WD
BB-104
TYPE: DEFENSE

	ATTACK	DEFENSE	STAMINA
ENERGY RING™: TEMPO		★ ★ ★ ★ ★ ★	
FUSION WHEEL™: TWISTED		★ ★ ★ ★ ★ ★	
SPIN TRACK™: 145 HIGH-PROFILE TRACK.			★ ★
PERFORMANCE TIP™: WD WIDE DEFENSE TIP FOR ENDURANCE.		★ ★ ★ ★ ★	★ ★

SPIRAL CAPRICORN 90MF
BB-102
TYPE: ATTACK

	ATTACK	DEFENSE	STAMINA
ENERGY RING™: CAPRICORN	★ ★ ★ ★	★ ★	★
FUSION WHEEL™: SPIRAL	★ ★ ★ ★ ★ ⤵	★	⤙
SPIN TRACK™: 90 WINGS PUSH DOWN TO STABILIZE THE SPINNING ATTACK.	★ ★		
PERFORMANCE TIP™: MF RIGHT RUBBER FLAT FOR INCREASED GRIPPING POWER.	★ ★ ★ ★ ★		★ ★

ON THE SHOW

BLADER: DR. ZIGGURAT

This Bey has a flat metal performance tip that helps it attack as well as increase its speed. It gets its name from the constellation Capricorn, which is said to look like a goat with horns.

ON THE SHOW

BLADER: FAUST
Special Move: Spiral Dimension

Dr. Ziggurat created this Bey using data from the Beyblade World Championship, and believes it to be the world's most powerful Bey. It can spin forever without stopping.

Don't worry — Gingka and his friends don't get to have all the fun. The beauty of Beyblade is that anyone with a Bey and a launcher can become a Blader. It's as easy as three . . . two . . . one . . . *LET IT RIP!*™

In this section, you'll get some real-world strategies for understanding your Beyblade, as well as suggestions for making the most of each match. Follow these six easy steps, and you'll be ready to battle Gingka . . . or any other champion Blader who wanders into your town.

BLADER'S BATTLE GUIDE

Face Bolt

Energy Ring

Fusion Wheel

Spin Track

Performance Tip

STEP 1: KNOW YOUR BEYBLADE

To be the best, you need to know your Beyblade inside out. Each Beyblade is made up of five major parts. Each component is equally important.

Face Bolt: The image on the Face Bolt shows the spirit of the Bey. This piece also holds all of the other parts together.

Energy Ring: This is attached below the Face Bolt. The Energy Ring determines the spin and direction of your Beyblade top. The Energy Ring also represents each Bey's spirit.

Fusion Wheel: In the center of the top is the Fusion Wheel. The shape of this wheel will determine how your Bey will attack and defend during a battle. Some wheels send a top on an offensive strike, while others will help a top repel an opponent with a defensive stance.

Spin Track: This piece determines the height of your Bey, and controls how the top will react when another top strikes it below the Fusion Wheel.

Performance Tip: The shape of this final piece controls how your top will move. It may spin in one place defensively, or aggressively circle the stadium in attack mode.

Gingka's father knows the most valuable component of any Bey. "The Bey's power is not the most important thing, Gingka. The most important thing is the Blader's spirit."

TYPE: ATTACK

GALAXY PEGASUS
W105R2F
BB-70

FACE BOLT

ENERGY RING™: PEGASUS II
★★★★★☆☆

FUSION WHEEL™: GALAXY
★★★★★★☆

SPIN TRACK™: W105
★★

PERFORMANCE TIP™: R2F
★★★★★★★

TYPE: DEFENSE

ROCK LEONE
145WB
BB-30

FACE BOLT

ENERGY RING™: LEONE
★☆☆☆☆☆☆

FUSION WHEEL™: ROCK
★☆☆☆☆☆☆

SPIN TRACK™: 145
★★

PERFORMANCE TIP™: WB
★☆☆☆☆☆☆

TYPE: STAMINA

HADES KERBECS
BD145DS
BB-99

FACE BOLT

ENERGY RING™: KERBECS
★★☆☆☆

FUSION WHEEL™: HADES
★★★☆☆

SPIN TRACK™: BD145
★☆☆☆☆

PERFORMANCE TIP™: DS
★☆☆☆☆☆☆

TYPE: BALANCE

DARK WOLF
DF145FS
BB-29

FACE BOLT

ENERGY RING™: WOLF
★★★★★★

FUSION WHEEL™: DARK
★★★★★★★

SPIN TRACK™: DF145
★★★

PERFORMANCE TIP™: FS
★★★☆☆☆☆

STEP 2: KNOW YOUR TYPE

Each part of a Bey is designed to make it strong in one of three areas: Attack, Defense, and Stamina.

Attack-types make fast, aggressive moves, but will stop spinning fairly quickly.

Defense-types can take a barrage of attacks without falling down.

Stamina-types spin for a long time, increasing your chances of outlasting your opponent.

Your Bey will come with a chart that shows you how strong your Bey is in each area. On the chart, the Energy Ring, Fusion Wheel, Spin Track, and Performance Tip are all assigned stars.

- ★ Red stars are for Attack.
- ★ Yellow stars are for Defense.
- ★ Green stars are for Stamina.

If there are more red stars than any other color, your Bey is an Attack-type. More yellow stars means you've got a Defense-type, and more green stars indicate a Stamina-type. A Bey with a more or less equal number of stars in each area is considered a Balance-type.

You can customize each top to change its strength in any area. Let's say you've got a Stamina-type with very weak attack power. You can switch out the Fusion Wheel for one with more attack power to boost your Bey's offense.

Once you get the hang of it, there are thousands of different combinations you can make. The choice is up to you!

BLADER'S BATTLE GUIDE

STEP 3: LEARN THE RULES AND STRATEGIES

The rules in a basic Beyblade match are pretty simple:

1. Face your competitor on either side of the stadium.

2. Launch at the count of "Three . . . two . . . one . . . 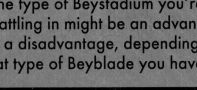"

3. The last top standing wins.

But the game becomes more complicated once you realize that you can use strategy to win. Here are some tips that will help you make the most out of any battle:

1. Know Your Opponent.

If you know which top your opponent is going to use, choose a top from your collection that has the best chance of beating it. Generally, Attack-types succeed against Stamina-types. Stamina types succeed against Defense-types. And Defense-types can withstand the aggression of Attack types. Of course, if you have a good Balance-type Beyblade, you'll be prepared in any situation.

2. Know Your Stadium.

The type of Beystadium you're battling in might be an advantage or a disadvantage, depending on what type of Beyblade you have.

New Beystadiums are released periodically, so the best thing to do is test them out and see what effect they have on your tops.

3. Customize. Knowing how to customize your Beys allows you to create an arsenal that suits your unique battle strategy. You might want a team of tops with different strengths. Or maybe you want a more aggressive team made up of all Attack-types. The beauty of customization is that if you don't like the results your tops are getting, you can always change them.

4. Develop a Launch Strategy. Practice launching your Bey from different heights and angles and see what happens. One popular strategy is called the Sharpshooter. It's a kind of sneak attack in which the top is quickly launched from an angle aimed right at the opposing top, catching it off guard. In a Concealment attack, the Blader hides the launcher under his palm and releases the Bey at the last possible moment. This allows the top to spin as long as possible in the Beystadium.

STEP 4: KNOW YOUR TERMS

Wondering what those numbers and letters after your Beyblade's name mean? Read on!

Numbers

Each Beyblade has two numbers. The BB number indicates the Bey is the same configuration as the original Beyblade top released in Japan. A B number indicates that the top may be a new configuration or something that has not previously been released.

The other number tells you about the Bey itself—for example, Storm Pegasus 105RF. The number 105 indicates how short or tall the Spin Track is, and RF tells you that it has a Rubber Flat Performance Tip (more on that below).

Letters

The letters in each Beyblade's name tell you what kind of performance tip it has. The kind of tip can make a big difference when you're battling. Below is a quick list of what some of the abbreviations stand for, as well as some info on how different tips can help you in competition.

B - Ball. A ball tip is round on the bottom, which helps it stay spinning longer. This makes it good for Defense.

BS - Ball Sharp. A sharp point on a ball tip. Good for Stamina.

D - Defense. A wider version of the sharp tip. Beys with this tip can recover more quickly from attacks.

ES - Eternal Sharp. A performance tip with a sharp, free-spinning bottom.

F - Flat. Flat performance tips are good for Attack.

FS - Flat Sharp. Common to Balance-type Beys. A flat tip with a smaller, sharper tip in the center that's good for offense.

GB - Gravity Ball. This performance tip increases your Bey's Stamina and stability.

HF - Hole Flat. A flat performance tip with a hole in the center. The flat bottom helps the Bey attack, and the hole is believed to give the top increased Stamina.

HF/S - Hole Flat/Sharp. With this performance tip, Bladers can change modes in order to counter their opponents. The flat tip is better for Attack; the sharp tip is better for Stamina.

RF - Rubber Flat. This tip will give your Beyblade an aggressive movement pattern. Often used in Balance type Beyblades.

S - Sharp. A performance tip with a sharp, pointed bottom. Good for Stamina types.

SD - Semi Defense. Good for Defense. Beys with semi defense tips will recover from attacks more quickly than Beys with sharp tips.

WB - Wide Ball. Beyblades that have wide balls on their tips tend to be strong in Defense. The wide tip makes the Bey harder to knock out.

WD - Wide Defense. This performance tip allows its Bey to spin for a very long time, increasing Defense.

WF - Wide Flat. This performance tip is a wider version of the flat bottom. Good for Attack.

STEP 5: CHOOSE YOUR GEAR

Every Beyblade comes with its own launcher. But you can use extra gear to maximize your top's performance.

Beyblade Metal Fusion Launcher Grip: You can attach your Beyblade's regular launcher to this device to give your top an extra boost of power when you launch. The handle opens up so you can store extra pieces for your top.

Beyblade Metal Fusion String Launcher: This device allows you to launch without your rip cord. Just attach your Bey, pull the string, and let it rip.

Beyblade Metal Fusion Stadium Pegasus Thunder Whip:
The slanted floor of this stadium allows Beys to spin super fast for extra excitement. This stadium comes in blue or yellow.

STEP 6: PRACTICE

"The more you get out there and battle, the better you become."
— Tsubasa

The best way to become an expert Blader is to get out there and battle! If you're lucky like Kenta, you might live in a town full of Bladers always looking for a challenge. But if you don't know any other Bladers, don't worry. With a parent's permission, you can practice online at www.beybladebattles.com

You can register on this site for free and create your own custom Beys. You get to choose from a variety of virtual parts to create the top of your dreams. Then you can battle online against the computer or live opponents. Controls on the screen allow you to direct your top's movements, speed, and launch. You can even boost its attack and defense powers.

Once you get the hang of it, you'll probably be eager to test your skills against stronger opponents. Then you're ready to enter a tournament. A good place to find information about tournaments is at www.beyblade.com.

If you've made it this far, you're ready to take on any opponent — even Lightning L-Drago. But remember, it doesn't matter how many times you win, or how many tops you have, or whether you've got the strongest Bey around. The most important thing is to have fun. After all, as Gingka says, "Having a heart that loves Beyblading makes a Beyblader stronger."

If you love battling and take good care of your Beys, you'll always be a winner. So get on out there and

レット・イット・リップ
LET IT RIP! ™